CHARLIE
and the Gold Mine

Learning What's Really Valuable in Life

Mary Hollingsworth
as

Professor Scribbler

retells the Parable of the Treasure Hidden in a Field

Illustrated By
Peeler-Rose Productions

Brownlow

Brownlow Publishing Company, Inc.

DEDICATION

To Carol —
Chief Scribe,
editor extraordinaire,
remarkable lady
and
my long-time friend,
with love,
Scribbler

6.95

A SPECIAL BOOK

For

_____

_____

From

_____

_____

Date

Dear Parents and Teachers,

Finding the real treasure of life in this disposable, throw-away society of ours is like digging for gold. We often have to shovel a lot of dirt before we find the nuggets that are worth keeping. Once we have found the gold, though, we should be willing to give up everything else of less value to claim it for our own.

Jesus told his disciples a story (or *parable*) that illustrates this point:

The kingdom of heaven is like a treasure hidden in a field. One day a man found the treasure, and then he hid it in the field again. The man was very happy to find the treasure. He went and sold everything that he owned to buy that field. (Matthew 13:44, ICB)

The important element of this story that we need to learn and that we need somehow to teach our children is that some things in life are worth more than others. And, further, some things are so valuable that we could give up everything else we own to get the more valuable item and still come out ahead in the long run. That's not an easy lesson to teach children in our materialistic world, we realize.

Charlie and the Gold Mine put this important concept into a child's format and on a level which can be easily understood. It is an allegory of the parable of the treasure in the field in a simplified story format, just as Jesus used for his "children" to grasp the concept.

There's plenty of suspense and excitement in this *Adventure of Charlie Wandermouse* to keep your child's attention and interest while he learns these valuable lessons being taught: (1) some things are worth more than others in life, (2) we should give up less valuable things in order to obtain more valuable things, and (3) keep digging into life — there's treasure to be found if you don't give up! Obviously, the spiritual implications of these lessons are profound for all of us.

Join Charlie and Professor Scribbler now with your child to look for buried treasure in *Charlie and the Gold Mine*. And keep in mind as you go about this hectic life that heaven will surely be worth it all.

The Publisher

Hello. I'm a writer named Professor Scribbler. And this is my best friend, Charlie Wandermouse — the world famous musician, traveler and explorer. This story tells us how Charlie found an old gold mine in the hills and all the risky things he had to do to buy it. Just turn this page, and get ready for adventure.

Now Charlie and I live at Flora Flittermouse's big boardinghouse on the banks of Flitterpond just outside Cheddartown.

It was a hot August day. We were drinking lemonade and fanning ourselves to stay cool when the telemouse rang.

To our surprise, it was my own sweet mom, Mother Mouse, calling from Killywash Kreek. Mother owns the Mouse Palace there and sponsors the famous old west musical in the Palace Theater. She wanted Charlie and me to come to Killywash and star in her next musical called "Cat Balooey."

It sounded like fun! So, we invited our two actor friends, Racey Red and Boo Boo Barb, to go with us and co-star in the play. Red and Boo Boo were pretty cheesey gals, but they have the strangest names, don't you think? Anyway, Mother said Charlie would get top billing as usual.

We packed Charlie's red Race-a-Cat Turbo and took off to Killywash Kreek. It was a happy trip through the mountains. We enjoyed the cool mountain air blowing through our whiskers. We sang our favorite songs, and even stopped for cocoa and cheesepuffs at some excellent roadside cafes.

When we arrived at the Mouse Palace, Mother Mouse ran out to greet us. She was looking perky as always with her frosted-grey fur shining in the sunlight. And she squeaked happily when she saw me. Mothers are like that, you know.

Now Mother Mouse is a very special lady because she's a writer, too. In fact, she taught me everything I know. She writes the musicals for the Palace Theater.

One day Charlie looked around Killywash Kreek and said, "Scribbler, wouldn't this be a great place to build the Charlie Wandermouse School of Music?"

"That's a great idea!" I said. "But where would you build it?"

"I'm not sure yet," said Charlie. "Let's go look for a piece of land." So, away we went.

We looked at land in the country and in the city. We looked uptown and downtown. We looked in the valley and on the mountains. We even looked at an old deserted school building, but Charlie didn't think it was quite right.

Finally, we drove up to a rocky old hill just outside of Killywash Kreek. I thought it was just another worthless bit of land and I was so tired. But we got out to look around anyway.

At the back of the land, we discovered an old mine entrance. So, we scampered in to nose around. Cats are not the only curious critters, you know.

Suddenly, Charlie said, "Scribbler, look at this!" pointing to a glittering streak in the wall of the mine.

"Mousetraps and catfur! It's gold!" I said. "This must be one of the Old West gold mines that has been forgotten." The more we looked, the more gold we found. The mine was loaded with it! We had found a rich, hidden treasure in the middle of a useless hill!

I said, "Charlie, there's enough gold in here to pay for building the School of Music, and a lot more!"

"Yes," said Charlie, "this land is very valuable. Let's go to the real estate office and buy it right now."

So, we hid the entrance to the mine, hopped in the Turbo and sped back to town. We were both so excited that our ears were wiggling!

We were shocked when the agent at Pied Piper Real Estate told us the price of the land. He said it would cost one million cheddars—that's mouse money, of course. He must have known, as the cowboys did, that there was "gold in them there hills."

Charlie and I looked at each other sadly. One million cheddars! That was more than both of us had put together—a whole lot more! Where could we get that kind of money?

Charlie said, "I know. We'll borrow it from the Cheddartown City Bank!"

So, we called our old friend Moolah Mouse at the bank. But all Moolah could loan us was 400,000 cheddars—less than half of what we needed.

"I've got it," Charlie said. "Let's sell some things we own. We can buy them all back when we get the gold out of the mine."

"That's a great idea, Charlie!" I said.

The Complete Works OF SHAKEMOUSE

So, we sold my favorite collection of the writings of the great William Shakemouse. We sold Charlie's highly valuable Stratavarimouse violin. We sold my platinum Poet of the Year statuette and we sold Charlie's huge collection of silver miniature mouster musicians.

All together, we made 300,000 cheddars from our sale. But we were still 300,000 cheddars short! What would we do?

Now we were desperate! So, I finally agreed to sell even my precious mousewriter that I use to make my living as a writer. Meanwhile, Charlie decided to give up his 9-inch, ebony grand piano. He was sad because he had composed so many wonderful masterpieces on that piano. And, as a last resort, we even sold Charlie's red Race-a-Cat Turbo!

It was a whisker-twitching experience, I must say. But, at last we had exactly one million cheddars! So, we rushed to the real estate office and bought the land.

We soon had dug enough gold from the mine to build the Charlie Wandermouse School of Music. And it was magnificent! We also had enough gold to buy back all the important things we had sold. And the other things? Well, we decided that some of our possessions were not very important after all.

By the way, the musical was a big success, too. Racey Red and Boo Boo Barb stole the show. And Mother Mouse received a Golden Mouse Award for writing the fantastic play.

On our way back to Cheddartown, we talked about our experience. I said, "Charlie, it was hard to sell my favorite things to buy that old hill, even knowing there was gold in it."

Charlie just winked at me. "Scribbler," he said, "sometimes we have to give up things that *seem* to be

valuable to us so that we can get what really *is* valuable. It's never easy, but the rewards are out of this world!"

I grinned at him and said, "Heavenly, you might say!"